The
WORRYSAURUS

For little River & Baby Sky...
may you always find a way to set
your butterflies free x
R.B.

For Akshay & Rian
C.C.

ORCHARD BOOKS
First published in Great Britain in 2019 by The Watts Publishing Group
First pubished in paperback in 2020

9 10

Text © Rachel Bright 2019
Illustrations © Chris Chatterton 2019

HB ISBN 978 1 40835 613 5
PB ISBN 978 1 40835 612 8

Printed and bound in China

Orchard Books
An imprint of Hachette Children's Group
Part of The Watts Publishing Group Limited
Carmelite House, 50 Victoria Embankment,
London EC4Y 0DZ

An Hachette UK Company
www.hachette.co.uk
www.hachettechildrens.co.uk

RACHEL BRIGHT

CHRIS CHATTERTON

The WORRYSAURUS

ORCHARD

On a hot and sunny morning,
under lovely clear blue skies,
A little Worrysaurus was
opening his eyes.

He brushed his tiny
POINTY TEETH,

then washed his

TOP AND TAIL.

He packed a little
BAG OF SNACKS
and set off on a trail.

He skipped along with happy legs,
across the golden sand,
And thought about the day that
he had plotted, sketched and planned.

A lovely **YUMMY** picnic, a **DELICIOUS** summer spread.

DINO BITES

Worrysaurus liked
it when he knew
what lay ahead.

But he hadn't gotten far, you see,
it hadn't been that long,
Before his busy head dreamed up
some things that might go wrong . . .

Had he made enough to **EAT** today?

And brought enough to **DRINK?**

This Worrysaurus often was a one to **OVERTHINK.**

What if I get **LOST?** he thought,
Or trip and have a fall?

His happy legs were slowing to a
SNUFFLY, SHUFFLEY CRAWL.

Worrysaurus liked it when he felt he
was prepared. Unexpected happenings...
they made him feel quite

SCARED.

So when...

. . . suddenly from nowhere, a lizard SKITTERED by

shouting in a squeaky YELP

and pointing at the sky,

"I think a STORM is coming!
I heard it's on its way!"

Well, that REALLY put a cloud
above his Worrysaurus day.

"A storm?" said Worrysaurus,
"When it's so dry and hot and sunny?"
BUT the news became a butterfly
that flittered in his tummy.

"I'm **NOT READY**

for the rain," he said.

"I haven't got my wellies!"

His teeth began to **CHATTER** and his knees — they turned to **JELLIES**.

And all the while, the sky was blue!
The sun it shone and shone.
But now his lovely picnic thoughts
were definitely gone.

Should he

find a cave

to shelter?

Or

RUN back home

and HIDE?

His little worry butterfly
grew very strong inside.

But then he thought of something
that his mummy liked to say:

"Oh, my
little Worrysaurus,

CHASE THAT BUTTERFLY AWAY!

Don't you worry now, my lovely,
you **MUST** try not to fret.
If it's not a happy ending,
then it hasn't ended yet."

So he reached into his bag just then,
to find a little tin.
It helped him with his worries -
it had **HAPPY THINGS** within.

A SPECIAL STICK,

his TEDDY NED,

a PEBBLE

My lovely little brave one
I'm so very proud of

and a LETTER.

And as he held them
ONE BY ONE...

so everything felt better.

Then he put away his tin
and all the worries
in his head...

FREED his little
butterfly for happy
thoughts instead.

"I'll stand
up **TALL**,
I can be
STRONG.

I'LL CHASE MY FEARS AWAY!

All is good and all is well

and everything's OK."

And with those
little wordlings

he calmed his
busy brain.

Since when the sun
is shining,

why worry it will rain?

So he shared his little picnic
with the lizard in the sun,
And they laughed at all their
worrying and **REALLY** had some fun.

Since when you're in the moment,
there's no need to run or hide.

And **THEN**
the only
butterflies...

...will be the ones outside.